A NOTE TO PARENTS

Reading Aloud with Your Child
Research shows that reading books aloud is the single most valuable support parents can provide in helping children learn to read.
- Be a ham! The more enthusiasm you display, the more your child will enjoy the book.
- Run your finger underneath the words as you read to signal that the print carries the story.
- Leave time for examining the illustrations more closely; encourage your child to find things in the pictures.
- Invite your youngster to join in whenever there's a repeated phrase in the text.
- Link up events in the book with similar events in your child's life.
- If your child asks a question, stop and answer it. The book can be a means to learning more about your child's thoughts.

Listening to Your Child Read Aloud
The support of your attention and praise is absolutely crucial to your child's continuing efforts to learn to read.
- If your child is learning to read and asks for a word, give it immediately so that the meaning of the story is not interrupted. DO NOT ask your child to sound out the word.
- On the other hand, if your child initiates the act of sounding out, don't intervene.
- If your child is reading along and makes what is called a miscue, listen for the sense of the miscue. If the word "road" is substituted for the word "street," for instance, no meaning is lost. Don't stop the reading for a correction.
- If the miscue makes no sense (for example, "horse" for "house"), ask your child to reread the sentence because you're not sure you understand what's just been read.
- Above all else, enjoy your child's growing command of print and make sure you give lots of praise. *You are your child's first teacher—and the most important one. Praise from you is critical for further risk-taking and learning.*

—Priscilla Lynch
Ph.D., New York University
Educational Consultant

D0028011

No part of this publication may be reproduced in whole or in part, or stored in a retrieval system, or transmitted in any form or by any means, electronic, mechanical, photocopying, recording, or otherwise, without written permission of the publisher. For information regarding permission, write to Scholastic Inc., 730 Broadway, New York, NY 10003.

Library of Congress Cataloging-in-Publication Data
Gelman, Rita Golden.
   More spaghetti, I say / by Rita Golden Gelman ; illustrated by
Mort Gerberg.
      p.   cm.—(Hello reader)
   "Level 1."
   Summary: Minnie the monkey is too busy eating spaghetti—all day,
in all ways—to play with Freddy.
   ISBN 0-590-45783-7
   [1. Stories in rhyme.   2. Monkeys—Fiction.   3. Spaghetti—
Fiction.   4. Humorous stories.]   I. Gerberg, Mort. ill.
II. Title.   III. Series.
PZ8.3.G28MO   1992
[E]—dc20   91-43181
                                             CIP
                                             AC

12 11 10 9 8 7 6 5   9/9
Printed in the U.S.A.   09
First Scholastic Printing, January 1993

More Spaghetti, I Say!

by Rita Golden Gelman
Illustrated by Mort Gerberg

Hello Reader! — Level 2

SCHOLASTIC INC. Cartwheel ·B·O·O·K·S·™

New York   Toronto   London   Auckland   Sydney

"Play with me, Minnie.
Play with me, please.

We can stand on our heads.
We can hang by our knees."

"Oh, no.
I can't play.
I can't play with you, Freddy.

Not now.
Can't you see?
I am eating spaghetti."

"Now you can do it.
Now you can play.

We can jump on the bed
for the rest of the day."

"No. I can **not**.
I can **not** jump and play.
Can't you see?
I need more.

More spaghetti, I say!

I love it.
I love it.
I love it.
I do.

I love it so much!"

"More than me?"

"More than you.

I love it on pancakes
with ice cream and ham.
With pickles and cookies,
bananas and jam.

I love it with mustard
and marshmallow stuff.
I eat it all day.
I just can't get enough.

I eat it on trucks,
and I eat it in trees."

"You eat it too much.
Won't you play with me,
PLEASE?"

"I can run in spaghetti.

And ride in spaghetti.

I can jump.
I can slide.
I can hide
in spaghetti.

I can skate on spaghetti,
and ski on spaghetti.

And look at this picture.
That's me on spaghetti."

"Spaghetti. Spaghetti.
That's all you can say.
I am going to throw
your spaghetti away.

I am going to throw it
all over the bed,
in the air,
on your chair,
on the floor,
ON YOUR HEAD!

Oh, Minnie,
that look on your face!
You look bad.
You look big.
You look green.
You look sick.
You look sad."

"You are right.
I am green.
I feel sick.
Yes, I do.
I think I will rest.
I will sit here with you."

"Let me take this away now.
I think that I should.

And then we can play.

Mmmmmmmm!
Spaghetti is good.

I love it.
I love it.
I love it.
I do.
I need more spaghetti.
I can't play with you."

"But **now** I can play.
I can play with you, Freddy."

"Not now.
Can't you see?

I am eating spaghetti."